Herbert Bell

Uncut stones

Poems

Herbert Bell

Uncut stones
Poems

ISBN/EAN: 9783744722711

Printed in Europe, USA, Canada, Australia, Japan

Cover: Foto ©Andreas Hilbeck / pixelio.de

More available books at **www.hansebooks.com**

UNCUT STONES

POEMS

BY

HERBERT BELL

LONDON
GEORGE REDWAY
1898

CONTENTS

THE GARDEN

INSIDE a garden grew a peach,
　　Soft and round,
With a blush upon its downy skin ;
　　It fell to ground :
And as it lay, two boys passed in,
　　And thus said one :
" It's mine ! "—and eating it the while—
　　" Take thou the stone ! "
Then said the other with a smile :
　　" Thy joy is gone ;
But mine doth only now begin,
　　In this the root,
From the threads of which the sun will spin
　　The tree, the fruit,
An endless joy beyond thy reach."

RUBY HEART

I

HE

O RUBY HEART! O Ruby Heart!
   Pride of a monarch's crown!
   From heaven to earth sent down!
Knit to my life, never to part!
   The bloody spear flew true
   To pierce him thro' and thro';
   I stayed it with my arm,
   Ere it had done him harm:
   The monarch lived, and me
   He gave the choicest gem
   From out his diadem;
   For, Heart, he gave me thee.

O Ruby Heart! O Ruby Heart!

 Pride of a monarch's crown!

 From heaven to earth sent down!

Knit to my life, never to part!

 At the moonbeam's kiss take wings

 And fly where the maiden sings!

 From Love's sweet cup she sips,

 Prays for her lover's lips.

 Now, Ruby Heart, away!

 Thy glistening wings unfold!

 Return ere break of day,

 With all her heart unrolled.

O Ruby Heart! O Ruby Heart!

 Pride of a monarch's crown!

 From heaven to earth sent down!

Knit to my life, never to part!

      [*Enter* RUBY HEART SPIRIT.

 Ah! yonder comes my faery heart,

 Gliding down the moonbeam's thread,

Fulfil to-night thy airy part,

While soft she dreams in downy bed!

RUBY HEART SPIRIT

I come from the land of fire,

Lord of my life, with whom I must die,

To perform thy every desire.

Command! at thy whisper I fly!

HE

I love the maiden Beatrice;

But know not if she love me too.

Away! and heart with heart converse!

Away! and tell me in a trice,

If she to me will e'er be true,

Come sorrow, woe, or sad reverse.

RUBY HEART SPIRIT

I will go! while in sleep she does rest,

I will tap at the door of her breast,

I will call out her spirit from thence,

To the sky we will speed us from hence ;

On some lonely peak of the mist

We will stand, where nothing can list

To the fluttering whispers of love :

Yes! high up in the heavens above,

Where the stars ever shine thro' the blue,

We will each to the other speak true.

HE

Fly then, my heart! fly away! fly away!

[*Exit* RUBY HEART SPIRIT.

II

He

Ah me! Come heart, and tell me of my love!

Her locks are steps by which men climb on high,

And angels come to men from heaven above;

Her lips are heaven's portals, and each eye

A gem. Her cheeks are gardens of the blest,

Bedecked with rose and lily. And all this

To be made mine by the impress of a kiss!

　　　　　　Made mine?

Oh, can it be? Ah no! all mortal dust!

The greedy earth at last will claim her own:

The steps will fall, the portals close, flowers must

To earth return, the gems no more be known.

Then art *thou* only dust, like to the rest?

Nay! thou art spirit. Those can ne'er be mine:

But spirit may! 'Tis deathless and divine,

　　　　　　Made mine!

　　　　　[*Enter* Ruby Heart Spirit.

RUBY HEART SPIRIT

Thine ! but not to be held by the ties

Of the flesh.   Let thy soul with her spirit arise !

For when voiceless on earth, to the heavens we fled,

Midst the clouds she was dumb ; on and upward

    I led :—

On, On ! till the light of the earth-star seemed

    dead ;—

Past the moon ! past the sun ! past the starlight

    we sped

To the centre of all, where the ether burns red

In the quivering heart, whence the sun globes are

    fed,

As each hangeth therefrom by a fiery thread.

There we lay with the wraith of a flame for our

    bed,

And her soul spoke to me in low whispers, which

    said :

"We are one! we are one! I am thine! thou art
  mine!
We are knit with the union of spirits divine!"
So she spake, and we slid down the thread of
  earth's sun.
She returned to her place, and our journey was
  done.

He

Yes! I know it, sweet guardian, I know it full
  well;
  For my spirit has burst all the bonds of the
    flesh
With tumultuous heave, like the ocean's first
  swell,
  Or Leviathan caught in a fisherman's mesh.
Oh! how could we sink to a union of clay,
When our spirits are one?   Sweet helper, away!

[*Exit* Ruby Heart Spirit.

III

HE

Come, maiden mine,

And let me sip

A draught divine

Of fragrant wine

From thy sweet lip !

SHE

Unchanged is the poet's tongue,

Tho' the world has grown so cold.

Thou dost sing as they sang of old,

When the world was warm and young !

HE

Yes, love ! for the mountain stream,

Sprung from the heart of earth,

Recks not the winter's birth ;

But flows, like the poet's theme,

A voice from the land of dream.

B

SHE

Ah ! but dead is the flower of love,

    On earth all unknown ;

    By angels alone

It is culled in the heavens above.

HE

    Yet the seedling is cast

        In the gloom

        Of Earth's womb,

        Tho' it bloom

    In the sunlight at last.

SHE

    E'en the seed is killed

    When the earth is chilled

        By the touch of the frost,

        And its promise is lost.

He

Sped from on High!

Immortal! Divine!

How can it die,

Tho' it only be mine

To grasp the reflection

Of heaven's perfection?

She

Oh! what wilt thou do,

To prove thou are true?

He

One kiss!

And we fly

Hand in hand

Thro' the sky,

To a land

Of bliss.

SHE

It is thine!

HE

Thou art mine!
The earth is no more;
Up! Up! let us soar!

SHE

Ah! we rise
To the skies,—
Two spirits made one!—
Past the belt of the world,
Where the stars float and swim,—
Each a glorious sun!—
Now their light has grown dim,
And, with pinions unfurled,
Flame-crowned ideals,—the visions we dreamed,—
Hover around us.   They are what they seemed.

HE

On ! On ! to the light we see far away !
-Our course is unfinished. Let us not stay !

SHE

Oh! the blaze and the glory, transcendently fair !
Surely God and His angels are waiting us there.

HE

Yes, love !

When the seed that is sown

To its fulness is grown

Up above!

SHE

It is done !

We are one !

I to thee,

Thou to me,

Must always be true.

THE BREATH OF SPRING

Oh! why from the earth flees the desolate
    gloom?

Why spring the flowers once more into
    bloom?

Why sing the birds in the branches above?

Love is the breath of the spring! it is Love!

        Love! it is Love!

Cold is the seed in the bosom of earth;

    Fair is the blossom unseen it contains;

    Lost to the world, to the light it remains,

Lost! till the breath of the spring gives it
    birth;

        Love! it is Love!

Hushed are the woodlands, the birds hold their
    songs ;
Sweet are their notes, but as yet they are still ;
What is the force which shall wake them from
    sleep ?
Wait ! what is this ? Oh, the heavenly thrill !
        Love ! it is Love !

Thoughts of high promise, uncertain of aim,
    Anchorless, rudderless, sink, and are lost !
    What ? must they ever by doubtings be
      tossed ?
Nay ! there is that which can waft them to fame :
        Love ! it is Love !

ELEMENTALS

UNDINES, GNOMES, SYLPHS, *and* SALAMANDERS

(*A Fairy Dance*)

I

SYLPHS

So we come ! so we go !
A breath in the wind !
So we come ! so we go !
A thought in the mind !

GNOMES

To and fro ! to and fro !
The scent of the fir !
To and fro ! to and fro !
The grasshopper's whirr !

SALAMANDERS

We are here! we are there!

The sheen of the moon!

We are here! we are there!

The sunshine at noon!

UNDINES

Everywhere! Everywhere!

A mist on the hill!

Everywhere! Everywhere!

A glint in the rill!

ALL

So we flit thro' the world!

UNDINES

The foam on the wave!

SALAMANDERS

The fire in Earth's crust!

SYLPHS

The blue of the sky !

GNOMES

The butterfly's dust !

ALL

So we flit thro' the world !

SUPERIOR SPIRIT

The world is a bundle,

Entangled and tumbled ;

Who will unravel

The threads which lie twisted ?

ALL ELEMENTALS

We ! we are the spindles,

The hands and the fingers,

Which spin from the bundle

The threads of its fortunes.

SUPERIOR SPIRIT

Rent is the awning
　　Of night !
Pearl of the dawning,
　　O light
Of purity rare !
Thy bosom is bare,
Thou standest revealed,
Pale from thy bath of foam.

The glow of thy blush breaks thro'
Thy gossamer veins of blue :
Wouldst thou be concealed ?
Snatch the mist from the rills !
Fly in this to the hills,
Over their tops to roam !

II

ALL ELEMENTALS

On the marge of the azure sea,
'Midst the forests of clouds we dance ;
Every song which the throat may sing,
Every sigh of the quivering string,
Every breath of the wind, are we :
Hand in hand thro' the loom of space,
Like the threads of the weft, we glance
In a wild harmonious race.

SUPERIOR SPIRIT

The threads of creation
By death can be broken ;
What then supplieth
The warp of the fabric ?

ALL ELEMENTALS

Life !—Life is eternal,

Unchanging, unbroken ;

Though severed the weft,

The warp is unfailing.

SUPERIOR SPIRIT

Swiftly is flying

  The day ;

Soul of the dying !

  O ray

Of glimmering sheen !

Thou stealest unseen,

From the depths of the crimson west.

 Kissing to rest

 The weary breast,

Thro' the night thou glidest ;

 But when morning

 Gives thee warning,

In the shade thou hidest.

III

ALL ELEMENTALS

Where the mirage keepeth
All things fair to see,
From every sphere reflected,
In golden light perfected ;
Where the ether weepeth
All the scents which be,—
Showers for ever tending
To a perfect blending,—
There ! there is our home,
High up in the dome
Of the circling world.
Thence ! thence do we come,
Like cloudlets unfurled.
The light is our car,
From star unto star

We fly ;

Hover ; alight ;

Then, filled with their sweets,

We hie

Back to the height

Where heaven's arch meets.

SUPERIOR SPIRIT

The threads are unravelled ,

The fabric is woven ;

What is the purpose,

When all is completed ?

ALL ELEMENTALS

This from us is hidden ;

Powers far above us

Ply their viewless stitches,

Knitting all together.

SUPERIOR SPIRIT

Ye are many ;
  God is one ;
And if any
  Work be done,
It is known
To Him alone,
Whence it wendeth,
Whither tendeth ;
  Only He
  Can decree
How it endeth.

"LIFE"

A LICHEN-CLAD abbey lay in ruins around,
Where tombs of the dead encumbered the ground,—
The signs of a race which had fallen and gone,
    Never to rise.

But there, in a spray of sunbeams which shone
On a tombstone, bathed a butterfly bright,
And flirted its pollen-sown wings in the light ;
    Life never dies.

SPIRIT AND CLOUD

I

A vapour asleep on the breast of night,

Kissed by the rays of the rising light;

Or a foam fleck, blown from the restless seas,

Tossed in the arms of the wayward breeze,

Is the love of the human soul! From its home

In ethereal flame, it has come

To linger awhile on the earth;

And man, like a mote in the sunlit air,

Has caught but a gleam of the brilliance rare

It brings from the place of its birth.

II

From the lonely tarn on cragbound hill ;
From the mere, which dreams in the silent shades
Of the trackless wood ; from ocean and rill ;
From the dewy earth, when the daylight fades,
The troops of the phantom vapours wake,
And out of the darkness break :
To the glistening dome they fly,—
Bodiless forms of a perfect grace,—
Until in the viewless depths of space,
Like a silvery web, they lie.

III

Oh, the joy ! which thrills thro' the radiant skies,

When spirits out of the darkness rise

To bathe in the fount of the boundless sea,

Which over the sands of eternity

To the verge of the earth-star flows ! Oh, the rest !

To be borne past the lonely crest

Of mountain, afloat in the breath

Of an infinite love, and to find the goal,

(So distant in life), in the perfect soul

    United again by death !

IV

As clouds adrift in the breezes' care

On crystal waves of luminous air

Meet clouds, and their beings melt into one ;

Or caught in the net of the new-born sun,

As he springs from the cave of night, they are

soon

Dissolved through the ether at noon ;

Or, when scattered abroad by the storms,

And suffused by the ruby-tinted rays,

Which pulse from the heart of the sinking blaze,

They weave their exquisite forms.

V

So spirits, controlled by the breath of love,
Mingle together like visions of dream,
And follow the paths of the stars above,
Now lulled by the thoughts of a voiceless theme,
Or whirled on the flames of impetuous wind,
Thro' the gates of the innermost mind;
Now stretching a rainbow thread
From a myriad quivering spirits spun,
Thro' the depths unbridged; or from sun to sun,
Like a brilliant nebula spread.

VI

When mountains awake from their forest beds,
And raise thro' the gloom their purple heads,
On the pearly wings of the new-born day
Come the lightsome mists, to dance and play
On heathery moor, or where forest glade
Has woven a carpet of shade.
The flowers, and the whispering trees,
Kiss the hem of their flying robes, and catch
In their joyous lips the jewels they snatch
From tresses unloosed by the breeze.

VII

To the cloud, as it sails thro' the azure sea,
Comes the cry of the fainting earth, " Wilt thou
    flee ?
Wilt thou flee to the place of thy rest far away,
And leave me to die ?   Oh, pity me ! pity, and stay
To fill me with life once more ! "   And the soul
Of the cloud is moved, and the goal
Of its hopes laid down to give
Its life ; to fall from the sky in rain :
So it suffers loss for another's gain,
And dies,—that the earth may live.

VIII

At the cry of despair, at the passionate call,

Which echoes the woe of the human soul

Through furthermost space, a spirit will fall;

Will sever itself from the perfect whole,

And leave the rest it has won, that the love

Of man's dream, exalted above

The range of his earthly desire,

May lift, like a star seen through clouds at night,

His hopes beyond the world's highest height,

On wings of mysterious fire.

IX

Not in the love of the earth-bound soul
Can the spirit find its longed-for goal !
Not in the throb of the human breast
Can it win the peace of a perfect rest !
Straight to the heart of the ultimate flame,
Far away to the home whence it came,
Must the spirit take its flight.
There, its breath is a note in the deathless strain
Which flashes over the glimmering main
In waves of celestial light.

HIBISCUS MUTABILIS*

* [This flower, which grows in certain Himalayan valleys, possesses the capacity of changing its colour. At night it is nothing but a knot of pressed green leaves. From dawn till ten o'clock the flower opens and looks like a snow-white rose, towards twelve o'clock it begins to redden, and later in the afternoon it is as crimson as a peony. The flower is sacred to the Asuras, who are virgins, devoted to the service of the goddess Chastity. The sun god (Surya) at the beginning of creation fell in love with an Asura; but his love was vain, the Asura would not listen to him. The natives call the plant "Lajjalu"—the modest one.]

NYMPH of the mountain vale, virgin flower!

Soul of a maiden fair!

Lajjalu!

Sweet is thy sleep in shadowy bower,

Fanned by the moonlit air,

Lajjalu!

Softly around thee cling pillowing leaves,

Hiding thy beauteous form,

Lajjalu!

Pale is the snow yon summit receives,

Fresh from the whirling storm,

Lajjalu!

Paler art thou at earliest morn;

Never a blush is seen,

Lajjalu!

Soon he will come, on ruby wings borne,

Lover he would have been,

Lajjalu!

Darting swift glances of fiery love,

Making thy blushes rise,

Lajjalu!

Surely thou lov'st him, riding above

Deep in the azure skies,

Lajjalu!

Or why is thy radiant purity
> Dyed with a crimson glow,
>> Lajjalu ?
Love, in the service of Chastity,
> Spirits indeed may know,
>> Lajjalu !

Perish Desire, that flies with the breath !
Cherished be Love, that lives after death,
> Lajjalu ! Lajjalu !

OPALS

I

EVEN as cloud-shadows, which on ocean seem
To cast a fleeting sadness, are the hours,
When in the cool I lie, and watch the showers
Of sunlight wake the birches' silver gleam
Among the gloomy firs, or hear the stream
Glide softly through the tangled grass and flowers,
Beneath wild rose, and honey-suckle bowers :
The hours when memory melts in present dream.

And once again, from foliage intertwined
With opening buds, one beautiful girl's face,
The spirit of the flowers, I dimly trace ;
Clear eyes and faintly blushing cheek, outlined
By clustered curls, falling in unfettered grace
About her neck and shoulders scarce defined.

II

Hers was no earthly face. Its spirit thrilled
And burnt, an inextinguishable flame,
Within the throbbing channels of my frame,
And all its inter-atomic spaces filled
With rapturous love and ecstacy, distilled
From iridescent lakes of light. No name
Can tell the change which o'er my being came,
The yearning passion time has never stilled.

In undimmed brilliancy on memory's gaze
That star-born beauty must for ever rise ;
As Heaven's mysteries revealed to eyes
Of man, irradiate the lingering days
Of earthly life, or sunset glorifies
The darkened waves with paths of golden rays.

III

Most sweet the song of birds in early spring,

When April thaws the winter-frozen notes,

And jets of music rise from panting throats,

And through the wakened woodlands fling

A passionate melody ; most ravishing,

The summer's hum, which pours soft antidotes

In sound-sick ears, and gently murmuring, floats

O'er scented fields, on pollen-laden wing.

But sweeter far the silent interchange

Of thought with thought, the voiceless harmony

Struck by the finger of eternity

From quivering heart-strings ; the communion

    strange

Of soul with soul ; the unrestrained range

Of inter-penetrating sympathy.

IV

Such was the mute conversing, which did knit
Our beings into one.   Ofttimes we lay
And watched our thoughts, like bubbles, steal
    away,
And upward float, with rainbow fancies lit ;
Or from our interwoven spirits flit,
Like painted butterflies in circling play ;
Or, hand in hand, through starry mansions stray,
Exalted by a bliss most exquisite.

O bitter pang of unattained desire,
Piercing the grosser flesh, which lingers still
Unquelled by Heaven's permeating fire,
Resist no more in vain the impetuous will
Of spirit's energy, and so fulfil
The destined peace, to which our souls aspire.

v

Somewhere in antenatal depths of light
She wanders now, while I am left to dwell
On earth, and from its fragile beauties tell
Her loveliness, or with prophetic sight
Rekindle in my thoughts the keen delight
Her yielding touch inspired, when first the spell
Of deathless love on our two spirits fell,
And drew us to the angel-trodden height.

Tho' our allotted bourns be sundered far
By the ethereal sun-sailed sea ;
Tho' all the æons of infinity,
Should come between : no space, no time, a bar
Can set to our perfected unity ;
For soul is drawn to soul, as star to star.

"O HAPPY SOUL"

O HAPPY soul! in those gardens blest,
'Mid deathless flowers for ever to rest;
   High up in the cool of the blue,
Pillowed and rocked on the sweeping cloud.
   Sweet Soul, to thy loved one be true!
Chained to the earth, by grief I am bowed.

List to my voice! on the breeze it will rise,
Sped from the earth ever up to the skies:
   "'Tis hard to be parted from thee,
Seen, but not seeing. Come from above,
   Sweet Soul, for thy pinions are free!
Comfort my heart with whispers of love!"

As moves a breath thro' the tops of the trees,

And music floats from the sensitive keys,

Behold! at my sorrowful call,

Stirred from repose 'neath shadowing wing,

On my soul thy spirit shall fall,

Lulling the wail of my heart's broken string.

THE FLOWER

WITH never a kiss from the breeze
In the cool of the shadowing trees,
   Nor a glimpse of the further blue ;
'Neath the gloom of an archway of brick
On a stone set in mud, that was thick
   With the ooze of a drain, it grew ;
      Yet perfect in every cell.

If darkness and filth have no power
To kill such a delicate flower,
   Can the flame of the Spirit's fire,
Which in realms of space had its birth,
Be quenched by the gloom of the earth ?
   Nay ! at last it will gain its desire,
      And rise to the height whence it fell.

THE TWO SOULS

I

I

Ah! Breath in the air!
While thy father, the Harpist Breeze,
In his sleep is chasing unseen
New dreams thro' the strings he draws
'Thwart the vault of the blue above,
Thou hast wandered far from thy home
And found in thy rambles a toy,
So unstirred at the heart's warm spring
As to seem but a lifeless thing
Which thy wayward fancy could deck
With garlands of delicate hue,
And leave at its pleasure a wreck;
To take thee again to the blue.

Ah! Breath in the air!

As the spirit of Life art thou come!

At thy touch earth trembles with joy;

Bedecked are the waiting trees

With a mist of gossamer green;

The throat of the throstle thaws

With a song of wonder and love.

Nevermore on fluttering wing

Shalt thou fly to the place of thy birth;

For to thee will the quickening earth,

With the throb of its new life cling!

II

Softly now thou breathest thro' the sleeping
woodland brake;

From thy flowing tresses waking buds their
sweetness take.

Lightsome birds, warm kisses snatching from thy
dewy lips,

Waft them to their lov'd ones wing'd with shaft
of melody.

Tinted mists of sunrise stealing thou dost bear
with thee;

From thy scattered treasure many an eager
flower sips.

III

Thy parent's voice comes sobbing from the void,
    calling thee,

It echoes on the sunlit mountain crest woefully;

And down the vale by laughing streams it sighs,

·   " Where ? Oh, where ? "

Thro' forest glades with many a whispered cry,

    " Art there ?—there ? "

It hastens onward over ocean's breast, far,
    O far !

To seek thro' ruby portals of the earth another
    star.

II

I

Ah! Breath of my Soul!
Sped is the light which illumined the earth,
Into the azure dome.　There let me fly,
　　Led like the airy swallow
Up, ever up by the rays of the sinking sun;
　　Far, O far, would I follow,
Thro' the depths of the sunset blaze,
Thro' the girdle of quivering haze,
　　And the cool of the yonder blue;
On, ever on, till the goal of my quest be won;
　　Till the dreams of my soul come true,
　　And the thoughts of my mind leap to birth,
Throbbing with burning life, never to die.

II

O thou fair shadow of dream,
Once seen ; but for ever supreme !
Thine image alone do I know,
As a wind-driven cloud in the clear
Of a pine-girdled mere :
But ever I pray it may grow,
Till the form of itself shall appear.
Many a year have I flung to the Past—
What though an æon I cast ?
I am sure of thy coming at last.

III

Tend thou the flower of my soul
On the calm of the heavenly sea!
Ah! suffer it not to decay!
But with delicate touch unroll
Its circle of petals each day,
Till its breast is unveiled to thee.
There glistens the pearl of my love.
'Tis thine, O 'tis thine,
Fair phantom divine,
To keep, till our meeting above.

IV

What beauties of earth can delight ?—
  Dark tarn on the mountain crest,
    Mirror of moon and star ?
  Swift stream in the tangled glen,
    Harping on many a stone ?
  Hot throb of the ocean's breast,
    Clasped by the breeze from afar ?
  Weird sough of the rushy fen
    Round hovel ruined and lone
'Neath the deepening shadows of night ?
  Moors, sweet with the gathered scent
    Of many a new-born flower ?
  Deep forest, with mossy beds,
    Raised on the spine-strewn floor
  Snow children, with drooping heads,
    Jewels from winter's store ?
  Spring, nestling with shy content
    In the blue of her misty bower ?

Glad fields, at a kiss from the sun

Upblushing a poppy red,

Turning their cheeks for more ?

Proud autumn, to labour brought

Heavy with fruit and corn ?

Day's ship, as with Viking dead,

Pushed in a blaze from shore ?

The moon and a star, distraught

In the net of the rosy morn ?—

From these can no comfort be won ?

Oh ! what joy my soul would have filled

Had I never beheld thy shape !

But now, with unrest never stilled,

Struggle ever I must to escape.

v

What can earth now be to me,

When my soul looks up to thee ?

Wings, tho' flight be scarcely known,

Still are restless to be free.

(So do larks, tho' from the nest

Close imprisoned in a cage,

Press the bars with panting breast ;

Flutter, with their wings scarce grown,

Eager from this earth to rise,

Singing upward to the skies).

Yes ! for in another age,

Sweeping on from space to space,

We have known in realms above

Spirits of exceeding grace,

And for me there waits afar

One, who from this distant star

Upward draws my thoughts of love ;

One, who flashes back again

Visions to my fainting brain,—

Visions of transcendent bliss,

Such as spirits only see.—

What can earth then be to me,

When my soul looks up to this ?

VI

Far away! far away! towards a goal unde-
  fined,
  Far away, on a sea of echoing wail
My soul rushes out, in its efforts to find
  A haven of rest, for its storm-tossed sail.
As the thunder-clouds trouble the heart of the
  world,
So the thoughts of my mind by their struggles
  are whirled ;
As the lightning of earth meets the flash from
  above,
So the flame of my soul, the embrace of thy
  love ;
As the storm from the world, so the strife from
  my mind
Melts away on the wings of the whispering
  wind.

E

VII

Breath of my soul !

   Love divine !

From the God-lit place of its birth,

Far beyond the confines of Earth,

   Thou bringest to me

A boon of ineffable grace.

   Reflected in thee,

A glimpse of that exquisite face

   Has been mine.

LOVE

Youth's golden day has passed away,
> All wasted!

The looked-for fruit has turned to clay,
> Untasted,

Struggling in vain to climb the steep,
> Nameless,

Man's praise and Heaven's reward to reap,
> Blameless.

The way is lost; hope, once so bright, is dying
fast;

The gloom has come; one day is numbered with
the Past.

> Do I sleep, or is it death?

I wake! I rise! a ray darts thro' the dead'ning
   night,
Hope reawakes ; the world again is tinged with
   light,
      Sighs another morning's breath.
   Love's ray it is which bids me rise,
   And leads me onward to the skies ;
   A golden ladder, stretching past
      Earth's highest crest,
   And upward, upward, till at last
      In Heaven rest !

Printed by BALLANTYNE HANSON & Co.
London & Edinburgh

www.ingramcontent.com/pod-product-compliance
Lightning Source LLC
Chambersburg PA
CBHW022155020726
47496CB00008B/2728